S0-ARN-874

Junior Great Books®

READER'S JOURNAL

3

Gratitude
Courage
Cleverness

BOOK TWO

This journal belongs to:

Great Books Foundation

Junior Great Books® is a registered trademark of the Great Books Foundation.

Shared Inquiry™ is a trademark of the Great Books Foundation.

The contents of this publication include proprietary trademarks

and copyrighted materials and may be used or quoted only with

permission and appropriate credit to the Foundation.

Copyright © 2015 by The Great Books Foundation

Chicago, Illinois

All rights reserved

ISBN 978-1-939014-81-8

2 4 6 8 9 7 5 3

Printed in the United States of America

Cover art by Rich Lo.

Text and cover design by THINK Book Works.

Published and distributed by

THE GREAT BOOKS FOUNDATION
A nonprofit educational organization

233 North Michigan Ave, Suite 420

Chicago, IL 60601

www.greatbooks.org

CONTENTS

CLEVERNESS

Gratitude

In this section of your book, you will read about characters who both give and receive thanks. Before you read these stories, think about this **theme question** and write your answer below.

Should people expect gratitude for doing something kind?

_____

_____

_____

After you read each story in this section, you may have some new answers to the question. Write them below.

_____

_____

_____

_____

White Wave

Chinese folktale as told by Diane Wolkstein

 Write about **a part of the story that you understand better** after the sharing questions activity.

_____

_____

_____

_____

_____

Write **the question someone else asked** that interests you the most.

_____

_____

_____

Write **the question you asked** that interests you the most.

_____

_____

_____

Second Reading

Write **something new you learned** from rereading or from doing an activity during the second reading.

_____

_____

_____

_____

_____

Write **a question you'd like to talk about more**. It can be a question you thought of already or a new question. You can write more than one question if you wish.

_____

_____

_____

_____

_____

Head in the Clouds

Choose one of the topics in the clouds and write or draw a picture about it.

Questions Kuo Ming's children might ask him

A picture of White Wave telling Kuo Ming she must leave him

Something you have taken good care of

How you felt at the end of the story

The focus question: _____

_____

Your answer before discussion: _____

_____

_____

A piece of evidence from the story that supports your answer:

_____

_____

_____ **Page:** _____

Your answer after discussion (explain how you changed or added to your original answer, and give evidence that supports your answer now):

_____

_____

_____

_____ **Page:** _____

Write your answer to the assigned essay question, and write three pieces of evidence from the story that support your answer.

Your answer to the assigned essay question:

Evidence #1 from page _____ :

> Your evidence can be a quote from the story or a summary of what happens in your own words.

How this evidence supports your answer:

> Explain how this piece of evidence supports your answer to the essay question.

Evidence #2 from page _____ :

How this evidence supports your answer:

Evidence #3 from page _____ :

How this evidence supports your answer:

Use these notes to write an essay. Each main paragraph of your essay should give a piece of evidence and an explanation of how it supports your answer.

 Write a question you had about the story that still hasn't been answered. Use this page to take notes for a short story that answers your question.

Your question:

NOTES

BEGINNING: Where and when does this story happen? Who are the characters?

MIDDLE: What problems or important events happen?

END: Are the problems solved? What happens to the characters?

Luba and the Wren

Ukrainian folktale as told by Patricia Polacco

Write about **a part of the story that you understand better** after the sharing questions activity.

_____

_____

_____

_____

_____

Write **the question someone else asked** that interests you the most.

_____

_____

_____

Write **the question you asked** that interests you the most.

_____

_____

_____

Second Reading

Write **something new you learned** from rereading or from doing an activity during the second reading.

_____

_____

_____

_____

Write **a question you'd like to talk about more**. It can be a question you thought of already or a new question. You can write more than one question if you wish.

_____

_____

_____

_____

_____

_____

Head in the Clouds

Choose one of the topics in the clouds and write or draw a picture about it.

A picture of the gardens and ponds around the manor house

Something you would ask the wren for

How Luba looks when she asks the wren to make her parents "as gods"

A note to one of the characters

Shared Inquiry Discussion

The focus question: _____

_____

Your answer before discussion: _____

_____

_____

A piece of evidence from the story that supports your answer:

_____

_____

_____ **Page:** _____

Your answer after discussion (explain how you changed or added to your original answer, and give evidence that supports your answer now):

_____

_____

_____

_____ **Page:** _____

 Write your answer to the assigned essay question, and write three pieces of evidence from the story that support your answer.

Your answer to the assigned essay question:

Evidence #1 from page _____ :

Your evidence can be a quote from the story or a summary of what happens in your own words.

How this evidence supports your answer:

Explain how this piece of evidence supports your answer to the essay question.

Evidence #2 from page _____ :

How this evidence supports your answer:

Evidence #3 from page _____ :

How this evidence supports your answer:

Use these notes to write an essay. Each main paragraph of your essay should give a piece of evidence and an explanation of how it supports your answer.

Write a question you had about the story that still hasn't been answered. Use this page to take notes for a short story that answers your question.

Your question:

NOTES

BEGINNING: Where and when does this story happen? Who are the characters?

MIDDLE: What problems or important events happen?

END: Are the problems solved? What happens to the characters?

Basho and the River Stones

by Tim Myers

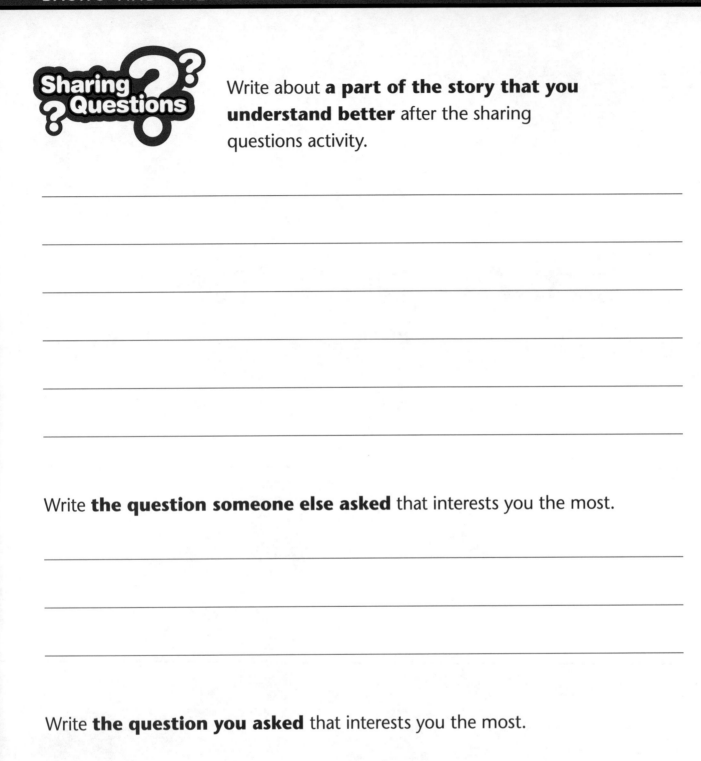

Sharing Questions

Write about **a part of the story that you understand better** after the sharing questions activity.

_____

_____

_____

_____

_____

_____

Write **the question someone else asked** that interests you the most.

_____

_____

_____

Write **the question you asked** that interests you the most.

_____

_____

_____

Second Reading

Write **something new you learned** from rereading or from doing an activity during the second reading.

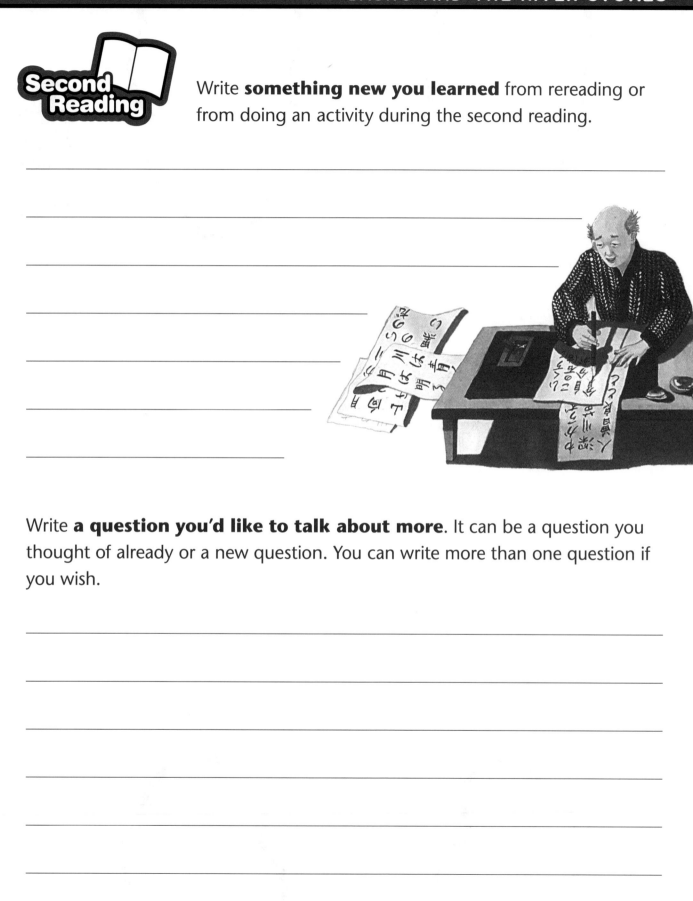

_____

_____

_____

_____

_____

Write **a question you'd like to talk about more**. It can be a question you thought of already or a new question. You can write more than one question if you wish.

_____

_____

_____

_____

_____

Head in the Clouds

Choose one of the topics in the clouds and write or draw a picture about it.

Your favorite character in the story

A picture of Basho stroking the fox's head

A time you enjoyed sharing food with friends

A picture of the fox hanging his head in shame

The focus question: _____

_____

Your answer before discussion: _____

_____

_____

A piece of evidence from the story that supports your answer:

_____

_____

_____ **Page:** _____

Your answer after discussion (explain how you changed or added to your original answer, and give evidence that supports your answer now):

_____

_____

_____

_____ **Page:** _____

Write your answer to the assigned essay question, and write three pieces of evidence from the story that support your answer.

Your answer to the assigned essay question:

Evidence #1 from page _____ :

Your evidence can be a quote from the story or a summary of what happens in your own words.

How this evidence supports your answer:

Explain how this piece of evidence supports your answer to the essay question.

Evidence #2 from page _____ :

How this evidence supports your answer:

Evidence #3 from page _____ :

How this evidence supports your answer:

Use these notes to write an essay. Each main paragraph of your essay should give a piece of evidence and an explanation of how it supports your answer.

 **Write a question you had about the story that still hasn't been answered. Use this page to take notes for a short story that answers your question.**

Your question:

NOTES

BEGINNING: Where and when does this story happen? Who are the characters?

MIDDLE: What problems or important events happen?

END: Are the problems solved? What happens to the characters?

STORY-TO-STORY CONNECTION
Gratitude

Write a letter as if you are a character from one story commenting on the way a character from another story showed gratitude. Before you begin, decide which character you are, and which character you will write to.

I am _____ .

I am writing to _____ .

Dear _____ ,

I **did / did not** like the way you showed gratitude toward
(circle one)

_____ .

> Give an example of the way the character showed gratitude.

continued

> Explain why you liked or did not like the way the character showed gratitude.

Sincerely,

_____

THEME INTRODUCTION
Courage

In this section of your book, you will read about characters who find and show courage in different ways. Before you read these stories, think about this **theme question** and write your answer below.

How does a person gain courage?

_____

_____

_____

After you read each story in this section, you may have some new answers to the question. Write them below.

_____

_____

_____

_____

The Monster Who Grew Small

by Joan Grant

Sharing Questions

Write about **a part of the story that you understand better** after the sharing questions activity.

_____

_____

_____

_____

_____

Write **the question someone else asked** that interests you the most.

_____

_____

_____

Write **the question you asked** that interests you the most.

_____

_____

_____

Write **something new you learned** from rereading or from doing an activity during the second reading.

_____

_____

_____

_____

_____

Write **a question you'd like to talk about more**. It can be a question you thought of already or a new question. You can write more than one question if you wish.

_____

_____

_____

_____

_____

_____

_____

Head in the Clouds

Choose one of the topics in the clouds and write or draw a picture about it.

A picture of the Monster the villagers imagined

A cheer the villagers could say to honor Miobi

A picture of the Monster when Miobi brings it to the village

Something the story makes you think of

The focus question: _____

_____

Your answer before discussion: _____

_____

_____

A piece of evidence from the story that supports your answer:

_____

_____

_____ **Page:** _____

Your answer after discussion (explain how you changed or added to your original answer, and give evidence that supports your answer now):

_____

_____

_____

_____ **Page:** _____

Write your answer to the assigned essay question, and write three pieces of evidence from the story that support your answer.

Your answer to the assigned essay question:

Evidence #1 from page _____ :

Your evidence can be a quote from the story or a summary of what happens in your own words.

How this evidence supports your answer:

Explain how this piece of evidence supports your answer to the essay question.

Evidence #2 from page _____ :

How this evidence supports your answer:

Evidence #3 from page _____ :

How this evidence supports your answer:

Use these notes to write an essay. Each main paragraph of your essay should give a piece of evidence and an explanation of how it supports your answer.

Story Organizer

Write a question you had about the story that still hasn't been answered. Use this page to take notes for a short story that answers your question.

Your question:

NOTES

BEGINNING: Where and when does this story happen? Who are the characters?

MIDDLE: What problems or important events happen?

END: Are the problems solved? What happens to the characters?

The Buffalo Storm

by Katherine Applegate

Sharing Questions

Write about **a part of the story that you understand better** after the sharing questions activity.

_____

_____

_____

_____

_____

Write **the question someone else asked** that interests you the most.

_____

_____

_____

Write **the question you asked** that interests you the most.

_____

_____

_____

Second Reading

Write **something new you learned** from rereading or from doing an activity during the second reading.

_____

_____

_____

_____

_____

Write **a question you'd like to talk about more**. It can be a question you thought of already or a new question. You can write more than one question if you wish.

_____

_____

_____

_____

_____

Head in the Clouds

Choose one of the topics in the clouds and write or draw a picture about it.

A picture of a thunderstorm on the prairie

What the inside of the cabin in Oregon might look like

Why you like or do not like this story

Something you're afraid of

The focus question: _____

_____

Your answer before discussion: _____

_____

_____

A piece of evidence from the story that supports your answer:

_____

_____

_____ **Page:** _____

Your answer after discussion (explain how you changed or added to your original answer, and give evidence that supports your answer now):

_____

_____

_____

_____ **Page:** _____

Write your answer to the assigned essay question, and write three pieces of evidence from the story that support your answer.

Your answer to the assigned essay question:

Evidence #1 from page _____ :

> Your evidence can be a quote from the story or a summary of what happens in your own words.

How this evidence supports your answer:

> Explain how this piece of evidence supports your answer to the essay question.

Evidence #2 from page _____ :

How this evidence supports your answer:

Evidence #3 from page _____ :

How this evidence supports your answer:

Use these notes to write an essay. Each main paragraph of your essay should give a piece of evidence and an explanation of how it supports your answer.

Write a question you had about the story that still hasn't been answered. Use this page to take notes for a short story that answers your question.

Your question:

NOTES

BEGINNING: Where and when does this story happen? Who are the characters?

MIDDLE: What problems or important events happen?

END: Are the problems solved? What happens to the characters?

Pierre's Dream

by Jennifer Armstrong

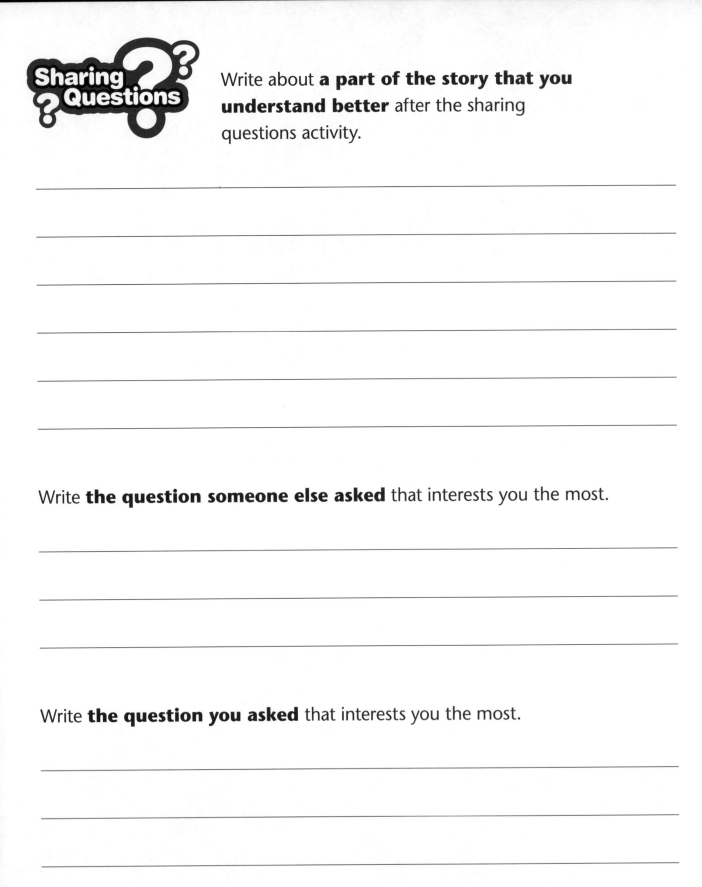

Sharing Questions

Write about **a part of the story that you understand better** after the sharing questions activity.

_____

_____

_____

_____

_____

Write **the question someone else asked** that interests you the most.

_____

_____

_____

Write **the question you asked** that interests you the most.

_____

_____

_____

Second Reading

Write **something new you learned** from rereading or from doing an activity during the second reading.

_____

_____

_____

_____

_____

Write **a question you'd like to talk about more**. It can be a question you thought of already or a new question. You can write more than one question if you wish.

_____

_____

_____

_____

_____

_____

_____

Head in the Clouds

Choose one of the topics in the clouds and write or draw a picture about it.

A conversation about Pierre between two people in the crowd

A picture of Pierre doing a death-defying feat

A picture of the circus folk thanking Pierre

Your favorite part of the story

The focus question: _____

_____

Your answer before discussion: _____

_____

_____

A piece of evidence from the story that supports your answer:

_____

_____

_____ **Page:** _____

Your answer after discussion (explain how you changed or added to your original answer, and give evidence that supports your answer now):

_____

_____

_____

_____ **Page:** _____

Write your answer to the assigned essay question, and write three pieces of evidence from the story that support your answer.

Your answer to the assigned essay question:

Evidence #1 from page _____ :

Your evidence can be a quote from the story or a summary of what happens in your own words.

How this evidence supports your answer:

Explain how this piece of evidence supports your answer to the essay question.

Evidence #2 from page _____ :

How this evidence supports your answer:

Evidence #3 from page _____ :

How this evidence supports your answer:

Use these notes to write an essay. Each main paragraph of your essay should give a piece of evidence and an explanation of how it supports your answer.

 **Story Organizer**

Write a question you had about the story that still hasn't been answered. Use this page to take notes for a short story that answers your question.

Your question:

NOTES

BEGINNING: Where and when does this story happen? Who are the characters?

MIDDLE: What problems or important events happen?

END: Are the problems solved? What happens to the characters?

STORY-TO-STORY CONNECTION
Courage

For each character:

- Fill in the bar labeled **B** to show how much courage you think the character had at the **beginning** of the story.

- Fill in the bar labeled **E** to show how much courage you think the character had at the **end** of the story.

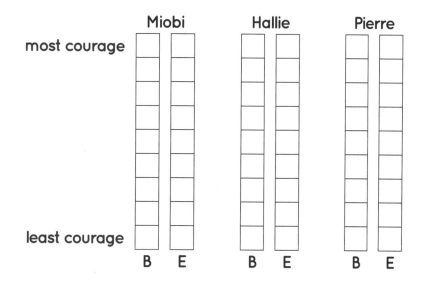

Now that you have filled in the graph, which character do you think gained the most courage, and why?

_____

_____

_____

_____

STORY-TO-STORY CONNECTION

THEME INTRODUCTION
Cleverness

In this section of your book, you will read about characters who do and say clever things. Before you read these stories, think about this **theme question** and write your answer below.

What does it mean to be clever?

_____

_____

_____

After you read each story in this section, you may have some new answers to the question. Write them below.

_____

_____

_____

_____

The Dream Weaver

by Concha Castroviejo

Sharing Questions

Write about **a part of the story that you understand better** after the sharing questions activity.

_____

_____

_____

_____

_____

Write **the question someone else asked** that interests you the most.

_____

_____

_____

Write **the question you asked** that interests you the most.

_____

_____

_____

Second Reading

Write **something new you learned** from rereading or from doing an activity during the second reading.

_____

_____

_____

_____

_____

Write **a question you'd like to talk about more**. It can be a question you thought of already or a new question. You can write more than one question if you wish.

_____

_____

_____

_____

_____

Head in the Clouds

Choose one of the topics in the clouds and write or draw a picture about it.

A picture of Gosvinda's house

A conversation you might have with one of the characters in the story

A picture of Rogelia being clumsy

A time you wished you could be more capable

The focus question: _____

_____

Your answer before discussion: _____

_____

_____

A piece of evidence from the story that supports your answer:

_____

_____

_____ **Page:** _____

Your answer after discussion (explain how you changed or added to your original answer, and give evidence that supports your answer now):

_____

_____

_____

_____ **Page:** _____

Write your answer to the assigned essay question, and write three pieces of evidence from the story that support your answer.

Your answer to the assigned essay question:

Evidence #1 from page _____ :

> Your evidence can be a quote from the story or a summary of what happens in your own words.

How this evidence supports your answer:

> Explain how this piece of evidence supports your answer to the essay question.

Evidence #2 from page _____ :

How this evidence supports your answer:

Evidence #3 from page _____ :

How this evidence supports your answer:

Use these notes to write an essay. Each main paragraph of your essay should give a piece of evidence and an explanation of how it supports your answer.

Write a question you had about the story that still hasn't been answered. Use this page to take notes for a short story that answers your question.

Your question:

NOTES

BEGINNING: Where and when does this story happen? Who are the characters?

MIDDLE: What problems or important events happen?

END: Are the problems solved? What happens to the characters?

The Man Whose Trade Was Tricks

Georgian folktale as told by George and Helen Papashvily

Sharing Questions

Write about **a part of the story that you understand better** after the sharing questions activity.

_____

_____

_____

_____

_____

Write **the question someone else asked** that interests you the most.

_____

_____

_____

Write **the question you asked** that interests you the most.

_____

_____

_____

Second Reading

Write **something new you learned** from rereading or from doing an activity during the second reading.

_____

_____

_____

_____

_____

_____

_____

Write **a question you'd like to talk about more**. It can be a question you thought of already or a new question. You can write more than one question if you wish.

_____

_____

_____

_____

_____

Head in the Clouds

Choose one of the topics in the clouds and write or draw a picture about it.

A worry that might keep you awake at night

A picture of the king watching Shahkro return to the palace on a donkey

A picture of Shahkro living in honor in his village

Your favorite scene in the story

The focus question: _____

_____

Your answer before discussion: _____

_____

_____

A piece of evidence from the story that supports your answer:

_____

_____

_____ **Page:** _____

Your answer after discussion (explain how you changed or added to your original answer, and give evidence that supports your answer now):

_____

_____

_____

_____ **Page:** _____

Write your answer to the assigned essay question, and write three pieces of evidence from the story that support your answer.

Your answer to the assigned essay question:

Evidence #1 from page _____ :

Your evidence can be a quote from the story or a summary of what happens in your own words.

How this evidence supports your answer:

Explain how this piece of evidence supports your answer to the essay question.

Evidence #2 from page _____ :

How this evidence supports your answer:

Evidence #3 from page _____ :

How this evidence supports your answer:

Use these notes to write an essay. Each main paragraph of your essay should give a piece of evidence and an explanation of how it supports your answer.

Write a question you had about the story that still hasn't been answered. Use this page to take notes for a short story that answers your question.

Your question:

NOTES

BEGINNING: Where and when does this story happen? Who are the characters?

MIDDLE: What problems or important events happen?

END: Are the problems solved? What happens to the characters?

The Emperor's New Clothes

by Hans Christian Andersen

Sharing Questions

Write about **a part of the story that you understand better** after the sharing questions activity.

_____

_____

_____

_____

_____

Write **the question someone else asked** that interests you the most.

_____

_____

_____

Write **the question you asked** that interests you the most.

_____

_____

_____

Second Reading

Write **something new you learned** from rereading or from doing an activity during the second reading.

_____

_____

_____

_____

_____

Write **a question you'd like to talk about more**. It can be a question you thought of already or a new question. You can write more than one question if you wish.

_____

_____

_____

_____

_____

Head in the Clouds

Choose one of the topics in the clouds and write or draw a picture about it.

A picture of the chamberlains pretending to hold the Emperor's train

A time you fooled someone

A picture of the medals that the king gave the swindlers

A note to a character in the story

The focus question: _____

_____

Your answer before discussion: _____

_____

_____

A piece of evidence from the story that supports your answer:

_____

_____

_____ **Page:** _____

Your answer after discussion (explain how you changed or added to your original answer, and give evidence that supports your answer now):

_____

_____

_____

_____ **Page:** _____

Write your answer to the assigned essay question, and write three pieces of evidence from the story that support your answer.

Your answer to the assigned essay question:

Evidence #1 from page _____ :

> Your evidence can be a quote from the story or a summary of what happens in your own words.

How this evidence supports your answer:

> Explain how this piece of evidence supports your answer to the essay question.

Evidence #2 from page _____ :

How this evidence supports your answer:

Evidence #3 from page _____ :

How this evidence supports your answer:

Use these notes to write an essay. Each main paragraph of your essay should give a piece of evidence and an explanation of how it supports your answer.

Write a question you had about the story that still hasn't been answered. Use this page to take notes for a short story that answers your question.

Your question:

NOTES

BEGINNING: Where and when does this story happen? Who are the characters?

MIDDLE: What problems or important events happen?

END: Are the problems solved? What happens to the characters?

STORY-TO-STORY CONNECTION
Cleverness

Choose characters from two different stories who showed cleverness.

Character #1: _____ **Character #2:** _____

Write a short conversation in which the characters say what they think about each other's cleverness. Put Character #1's lines in the speech bubbles on the left, and Character #2's lines in the speech bubbles on the right.

continued

STORY-TO-STORY CONNECTION: Cleverness (continued)

REFLECTING ON
Junior Great Books

Think about the time you've spent working on Junior Great Books this year. What skills have you learned, and what will you take away from the experience?

Which of these skills do you think you've improved the most by doing Junior Great Books? Put a check (✓) next to each skill you improved, and explain how you improved the skill.

☐ Asking questions about what I read _____

_____

☐ Thinking hard about the meaning of what I read _____

_____

☐ Backing up ideas with evidence _____

_____

☐ Listening and responding to other people's ideas _____

_____

☐ Respecting other people's ideas _____

_____

continued

REFLECTING ON (continued)

How have you used one of these skills outside of Junior Great Books (in another school subject, at home, or with your friends)?

_____

_____

_____

What was your favorite story in Junior Great Books, and why?

_____

_____

_____

What will you remember most about doing Junior Great Books this year?

_____

_____

_____

Have a question, a comment, or something else you want to tell the people who create Junior Great Books? E-mail us at **ask@greatbooks.org**.